First American Edition 1997 by Kane/Miller Book Publishers
Brooklyn, New York & La Jolla, California

Originally published in 1996 in Germany under the title *Die Riesin*
by Verlag Heinrich Ellermann, Munich, Germany

Library of Congress Cataloging-in-Publication Data

Hasler, Eveline.
[Riesin. English]
The giantess / Eveline Hasler : [illustrated by] Renate Seelig. — 1st American ed.
p. cm.
"Originally published in 1996 in Germany under title Die Riesin
by Verlag Heinrich Ellermann, Munich, Germany."
Summary: Through the friendship of a kind neighbor, a young
giantess discovers that her height is no obstacle to happiness.
ISBN 0-916291-76-6
[1. Fairy tales. 2. Size—Fiction. 3. Self-acceptance—Fiction.]
I. Seelig, Renate, ill.   II. Title.
PZ8.H2564Gi   1997 [E]—dc21   97-16637

Printed and bound in Singapore by Tien Wah Press Ltd.
1 2 3 4 5 6 7 8 9 10

The GIANTESS

Eveline Hasler · Renate Seelig

Translated by Laura McKenna

A CRANKY NELL BOOK

 Kane/Miller Book Publishers

Brooklyn, New York & La Jolla, California

Once upon a time there was an exceptionally tall young woman—a giantess—named Emmeline. She lived in seclusion at the edge of the forest for fear that her extraordinary height would scare people. She remembered the time she surprised a woman picking mushrooms, who upon seeing Emmeline, ran away in complete terror.

Emmeline would often look out her upstairs window and think about what her mother, a woman of average height, had told her:

"A giant? It's fine to be a giant, but a giantess? That won't do. Other women won't want to be your friend, and no man, since men expect women to look up *to them*, will ever fall in love with you. You will have a lonely life."

As it happened, a young woodsman built a log cabin at the edge of the forest, just opposite Emmeline's house. He would often look up in her direction.

He liked the face he saw high up in the window
and soon began to wave each time he saw her.

Emmeline would wave back shyly and then watch the woodsman as he went off to work.

"If only someone would come along who was like me," she sighed.

As time passed, the woodsman
would exchange a few words with
her whenever he passed by.

At the end of February, as the days began to get longer, the woodsman heard that a carnival was in town. "I'll ask my neighbor if she'd like to go," he decided.

However, when he arrived home that night, he didn't see Emmeline in the window. He knocked on her front door, but she didn't answer. He rang the bell, but no one came. Finally, he pushed the door open a little and peeked into the house.

Fast asleep on an enormous bed lay Emmeline . . .
to his surprise and astonishment . . . a giantess!
Her face was even prettier than the one in the
window, and she was smiling, as if in the middle of
a sweet dream.

Very quietly, so as not to wake her, he closed the
door and went home. He decided that what he had
seen would remain his secret.

The next morning the woodsman stood under Emmeline's window. "Hello, neighbor!" he cried out. "There's a carnival in town. Would you like to meet me there? I bet I'll recognize you even with your mask on! Please say you will . . ."

"Oh!" she replied timidly. "A carnival? I'm not sure what I could go as . . ."

"Don't worry!" laughed the woodsman. "At a carnival, you can be anything you wish! I'm sure you'll see everything there from elves and fairies to witches and giants."

"Hmm," thought Emmeline. "This might be the perfect opportunity for me to be among people. Everyone will just think I'm *dressed* as a giantess . . . and for once no one will be afraid of me."

So Emmeline did go to the carnival. How her face lit up when she saw all the costumes! She mingled with the masked crowd and felt at ease with everyone . . .

. . . the witches and gypsy girls, the pirates and the elves.
Many of the people, particularly the children, stopped and
looked up to admire her.

One little girl called out, "I like you, Giantess!
If we were at the zoo, I could get up on your shoulders
and kiss the giraffe on the nose!"

Then a young boy yelled out to her, "If we went to
the circus, I could sit on your shoulders and be able
to see everything!"
    Emmeline closed her eyes, smiled, and for a moment
imagined herself at the zoo and the circus with the two children.

"I too would be happy to have you around," said a farmer.
"A couple of tiles on my barn roof are loose, and the gutter
is all blocked up. It would be so simple for you to fix everything!"

Emmeline closed her eyes once again and this time pictured
herself repairing the roof. It made her feel good to think that
people could benefit from her great height.

Suddenly a hush fell over the crowd. Coming over the bridge, and smiling at Emmeline, was another giant! The crowd made way for him.

Taking each other's hand, Emmeline and the giant danced a Giant's Dance. The crowd smiled and clapped with delight.

Oh, how Emmeline loved to dance! And what
a joy it was to look straight into someone's eyes.
The beautiful eyes that looked back at her from
behind the mask reflected the forest and the clouds
and the blue of the sky. "I'm so happy to have finally
met someone my own size!" thought Emmeline.

Just then a little girl pulled at the giant's trousers in order to see if his legs were real. But the giant, who in fact was standing not on his own legs but on stilts, teetered and then toppled to the ground with a crash.

The giant, of course, was not a giant at all, but rather a man of average size. And when Emmeline recognized him to be her neighbor, tears ran down her cheeks.

"What about you, Giantess?" one of the children asked.
"Are you real at least?"

Emmeline wiped the tears away with the back of her hand.
She felt angry and sad and brave all at the same time.

She looked around the crowd, and then in a loud voice
exclaimed, "I'm going to let you all know my secret.
Yes, I am a real giantess. I live alone at the edge of the forest
so I won't scare anyone."

She held her breath, expecting people to run away in fear.
But no one did.

"You're real?" asked a small boy. "That's fantastic!"

The woodsman, feeling ashamed, had gone to the back of the crowd. But hearing the giantess, he too felt brave, and he moved towards her.

"Now I'd like to share a secret with you," he said. "For quite some time I've known you are a giantess. But that has never been a reason for me not to like you. You remind me of my friends, the trees. They're tall too! And, if you'd like, tomorrow I'll show them to you."

And so the next day, Emmeline and the young woodsman took a walk together through the forest. Hand in hand.